To Honey and Leon,
and to any dog looking for a forever home
—A.C. & G.S.

All rights reserved. Published in the United States by Random House Children's Books, a division of
Penguin Random House LLC, New York.

Random House and the colophon are registered trademarks of Penguin Random House LLC.

Visit us on the Web! rhcbooks.com

Educators and librarians, for a variety of teaching tools, visit us at RHTeachersLibrarians.com

Library of Congress Cataloging-in-Publication Data is available upon request.

ISBN 978-0-399-55800-9 (trade) — ISBN 978-0-399-55801-6 (lib. bdg.) — ISBN 978-0-399-55802-3 (ebook)

MANUFACTURED IN CHINA

10 9 8 7 6 5 4 3 2 1

First Edition

Random House Children's Books supports the First Amendment and celebrates the right to read.

HONEY & LEON TAKE THE HIGH ROAD

by
Alan Cumming

illustrated by
Grant Shaffer

Random House New York

SEARCH & DESTROY

Honey and Leon live with their two dads in the East Village of New York City. Can you find them?

Honey and Leon love to dress up. . . .

But it isn't just dressing up for fun. You see, their dads go away a lot, traveling for work. An *awful* lot. It used to make Honey and Leon so sad, until finally they decided to follow them, in disguise! And not only could they do their doggie duty and protect the dads, but they also had fun!

One day the dads and Honey and Leon
finished off their shopping. . . .

Just as they left
the bagel shop . . .

When they got home, the dads dried Honey and Leon with their special rainy-day towels, then played tug-of-war with them. It was almost worth getting caught in the rain for!

But then . . .

GRRRr

RAAAARRRR!

. . . Honey and Leon
heard a familiar sound!

SQuEaK SQuEaK SQuEaK

"Where on earth can they be going this time?" asked Honey.
"A place where you need rain hats, walking boots, umbrellas and bug cream," said Leon. "They're going somewhere cold and wet! And with bugs!"

"What about the bagels?" Honey replied.

"That's easy! Cold and wet and buggy places don't tend to have gluten-free everything bagels *or* tofu spread when you need them, do they?"

Later that evening the dogs found a clue.

Honey caused a diversion as Leon nabbed the tickets.

Leon's little paws made using a computer very easy.

The next day they were off!

When the dogs fell asleep, the dads came to check on *them*!
You see, the dads know that Honey and Leon follow them
all round the world! But they don't let on that they know
because they understand that dogs are only really happy when
they're protecting their humans.

When the plane landed, Honey and Leon jumped
in a London cab and followed the dads.

But the dads' journey wasn't over.

In the train's restaurant car,
Leon spied a looming disaster!
One of the dads was vegan,
and the soup he'd ordered
had ham in it! Honey and
Leon sprang into action!

Crisis averted! Everyone slept soundly that night.

The next morning they arrived in Edinburgh!

Of course, danger was never far off.
Honey and Leon were kept busy!

The next morning the dads were off again!

And that afternoon there was even more traveling!

The dads had come to stay on an island called Barra.

The next morning Honey went on her date
with Coll, leaving Leon in charge of the dads
and Granny all by himself.

Suddenly a blanket of fog descended, covering everything and everyone! How would they all get home? Leon knew it was up to him to save the day. But how?

Suddenly . . .

GLUTEN-FREEEE

Leon barked as he ran to guide everyone home safely . . .
but he did so in a Scottish accent so they wouldn't know it
was him!

A few days later it was time to leave the island
and return home to New York City.

Are you okay, Honey?
Oh, Leon, better to have lost in love than never to have loved at all.

After a long journey, they arrived back in New York.

Honey and Leon jumped in a cab and raced home.

When the dads arrived home, Honey and Leon leapt into their arms as though they hadn't seen them for a week!

Of course, the dads knew better. But this was a secret they were never going to tell.